KT-489-790

BOB
to the Rescue

JAMES BOWEN
& GARRY JENKINS

ILLUSTRATED BY
GERALD KELLEY

RED FOX

To Brendon Winters and his boys, Ethan & Hamish. This one's for you guys!! – J.B.
To the memory of Eric, my father and friend. – G.J.

BOB TO THE RESCUE
A RED FOX BOOK 978 1 782 95485 9

Published in Great Britain by Red Fox, an imprint of Random House Children's Publishers UK A Penguin Random House Company

Penguin
Random House
UK

This edition published 2015
10 9 8 7 6 5 4 3 2 1

Text copyright © James and Bob Limited and Connected Content Limited, 2015. Illustrations copyright © Random House Children's Publishers UK, 2015. Illustrated by Gerald Kelley. All photographs copyright © Garry Jenkins, 2015. The right of James Bowen, Garry Jenkins and Gerald Kelley to be identified as the authors and illustrator of this work has been asserted in accordance with the Copyrights, Design and Patents Act 1988. All rights reserved. No part of this publication may be reproduced, stored in a retrieval system, or transmitted in any form or by any means, electronic, mechanical, photocopying, recording or otherwise, without the prior permission of the publishers. Red Fox Books are published by Random House Children's Publishers UK, 61-63 Uxbridge Road, London, W5 5SA.

www.randomhousechildrens.co.uk www.randomhouse.co.uk
Addresses for Penguin Random House companies can be found at www.randomhouse.co.uk/offices.htm
The Random House Group Limited Reg. No. 954009
A CIP catalogue record of this book is available from the British Library. Printed in China.

Penguin Random House is committed to a sustainable future for our business, our readers and our planet. This book is made from Forest Stewardship Council® certified paper.

FSC
www.fsc.org
MIX
Paper from
responsible sources
FSC® C018179

Hello. I'm Bob the Street Cat. I used to be homeless, but then I met my best friend James, who gave me somewhere lovely and warm to live.

This is the story of how I met another of my friends.

It was the perfect autumn afternoon in the park. James was strumming his guitar while I watched the birds in the trees. The sun was shining and we were both as happy as could be.

Just then I heard a strange noise coming from the bushes. It sounded like a whimper, like someone or something was upset . . . "I wonder what it could be?" I thought, so I went to take a closer look.

I heard the sound again, and saw something white
disappearing into a bush ahead.
"Who's there?" I asked. But there was no reply.

I decided to follow it into the bush – and found a little white puppy! He was shivering and his big hazel eyes were filled with fear.

"My name is Bob. What's yours?" I said in a friendly voice.
But he just rocked from side to side, looking really scared.
I stepped towards him but he snapped at me. I was annoyed.
"Silly boy," I thought. "I was only trying to help."

Just then James called me.
"Bob, Bob. Time to go home, mate."
But I was worried about the puppy.
He might be lost or abandoned. He was all alone.

Later, back at home, I stared out into the dark, rainy night. The wind was howling. I watched to see if the little puppy would walk past with his owner. But the street was empty. There was no sign of him. He must have still been in the park.

I knew just how that poor puppy felt. I had once been homeless, forced to sleep out in the cold. I remembered how frightened and hungry I had been. I remembered how I had wished for a kind soul to help me. I knew what I must do.

Just then the doorbell rang and I took my chance. I slipped through James's legs and ran downstairs before he realised.

I had to be quick – if I wasn't back soon I knew James would come looking for me.

Out in the dark, I felt afraid. The poor puppy must be
frightened too, and cold and hungry. I saw an open bin,
so I jumped up and found a leftover sausage for him.

I ran to the park to find him.
"Hello?" I said, peering into the bushes. Soon the puppy
poked his head out. He looked even more frightened now.

I pushed the sausage towards him. He sniffed it but didn't eat it. "Come on, you've got to eat," I said. He just growled at me – he was still scared and didn't understand that I was a friend. There was nothing more I could do. I was freezing and my fur was soaked through. I headed home, feeling sad.

Suddenly I heard a loud **"WOOF, WOOF, WOOF!"**

It was a big dog, running towards me. I ran for the park gate.

I could sense it closing in on me.
I just shut my eyes.

All at once, I heard a yelping sound and the big dog turned away from me.

Out of the shadows a ball of white fur appeared, snapping and snarling at the big scary dog. It was the puppy!

The big dog actually looked
frightened of the puppy. I was
frozen to the spot.

And then I saw James – he was running towards us.
"Hey! Get lost!" he shouted, waving his arms at the big dog.
It turned and ran away.

My heart was racing.
I could hardly breathe.
I jumped straight into
James's arms.

"Bob! What on earth are you doing out here
at this time of night?" he said.

"And who is this brave little fella?" he asked.
The puppy gazed up at James. He wasn't scared
any more and knew we were his friends.
"Let's get you a meal and a warm bed.
We will find your home in the morning."

Back at home the puppy gobbled up a plate of food in a flash.
He then snuggled up alongside me next to the radiator.
We all slept very soundly that night.

The next morning James got us up early. "Time to find your home," he said to the puppy. "We'll see if they can help at the police station."

On the way we came across a poster. The puppy
in the picture looked just like my new friend.
"You clever boy, Bob," James said, scribbling down a
phone number. "That's why you went back to the park.
You guessed he was lost."

James rang the number and we soon headed off. We knocked
on the door of a big house and a nice lady answered.
"Patch!" she shouted when she saw the puppy.

Then she called, "Jenny! Look who's here!"
and a little girl came running down the stairs.
"Patch! I thought I'd lost you for ever," she cried, kissing
and cuddling the little dog. Patch yelped and wagged his
tail with joy. He couldn't stop licking her face.

"Bob to the rescue," said James.
I felt so proud.

Sometimes I see my friend Patch in the park. We run off into the bushes to play. Jenny and her mummy are never far away. Together we make sure that Patch never gets lost again.

Bob
AND
James

My Name is BOB

My Name is
BOB

JAMES BOWEN
& GARRY JENKINS

A MOVING AND UPLIFTING TALE
THAT WILL MELT YOUR HEART

A STREET CAT NAMED BOB

GERALD KELLEY

ABOUT JAMES AND BOB

In March 2007 James Bowen, a busker, found a ginger tom cat sitting injured in the hallway of the North London block of flats where he lived. Realising that he was a homeless stray, James gave the cat somewhere to sleep and spent most of the little money he had on medicine to heal his wounds.

He nursed the cat back to health, expecting him to return to the streets. But Bob, as James had by now named him, had other ideas. He started following James around, even jumping on a bus one morning as his new friend headed to work in Covent Garden.

Soon the striking-looking pair had become popular figures on the streets of London, where people gave them money and presents. James had been homeless too and was trying to make a new life for himself. Together, he and Bob helped each other to find happiness and hope again.

In 2012 *A Street Cat Named Bob*, a book about their adventures, written by James with my help, was published. It became a best-seller around the world and has been trtaranslated into more than thirty languages. We have since written two more adult books, *The World According to Bob* and a Christmas story, *A Gift from Bob*, as well as a children's picture book, *My Name Is Bob*. Today, James and Bob still live together in London, where they raise money for charities that help animals and the homeless. Plans to turn their story into a movie are at an advanced stage.

Garry Jenkins

London, 2015